Clearwater Girl

Written and Illustrated by:

Diana Clark

To order additional copies, please contact us.
BookSurge, LLC
www.booksurge.com
1-866-308-6235
orders@booksurge.com

This book is dedicated lovingly to my daughter Jamie.

Acknowledgment:

Thank you God for blessing me with so many wonderful people. I would like to thank my family and friends for their support and encouragement: Jamie Clark, Riaz Bandali, Irene Locker, Ingrid Clark(Mama), Heidi and Teddy Bamer, Sylvia Smith, Liz Orred, Sigrid Gatens(Scanner Queen), Marilyn Tomlin(Proofer#1), Erik Krema(Proofer#2), Janet Wooldridge(Proofer#3), Michael David, Douglas Smith, and Kevin Gumke (Photographer).

With a streak of blonde in her raven hair, Clearwater Girl was, in her mind, clearly different.

She worked alongside her mother, as all the girls in her village did. Clearwater Girl always finished her chores before playing.

When it was time for fun, she played with all her friends.
All the children were included during playtime.

Clearwater Girl spent many happy days with her friends.

Clearwater Girl disliked the blonde streak in her hair. She told her mother it made her feel different from the other girls. Her mother asked her to take a closer look at everyone and she would see that we all have our differences.

Clearwater Girl thought about what her mother had told her, but all she could think of was that all her friends had beautiful dark hair and that just made her want to get rid of the strands even more.

One day, Clearwater Girl rode her paint horse down to the stream.

She had only one thing in mind.

Near the stream grew blackberry bushes. She sat on the ground and started to pick the berries.

Clearwater Girl was feeling very excited to know she would soon be rid of the blonde streak in her hair.

After she had picked a basket full of berries, she began to crush them into her hair.

Her paint horse waited patiently by her side.

She looked into the clear stream at her reflection. The black juices had completely covered the blonde streak and her hair was now jet-black.

This brought a big smile to her face. She was very pleased.

Clearwater Girl jumped for joy! She was very happy. She finally would look like everyone else in her village.

Clearwater Girl was so busy looking at herself, she did not notice the change in the weather.

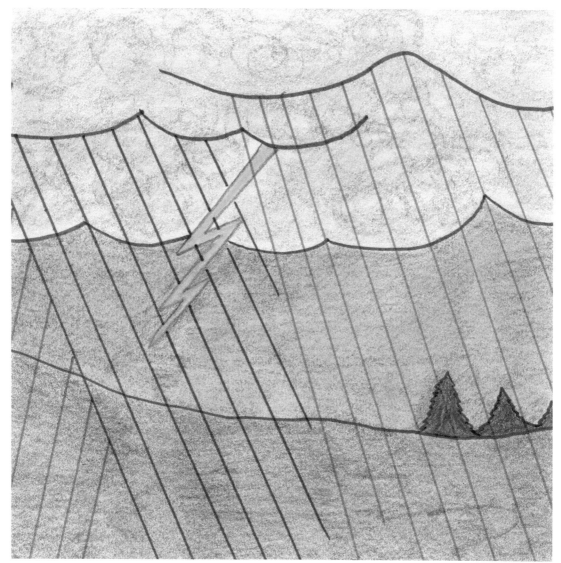

The beautiful sunny day was gone and a big storm was fast approaching. She jumped onto the back of her paint horse and rode swiftly towards her village.

She was riding fast, but the rain had begun to wash the blackberry juice down her face in big streaks of black.

When she arrived back home, she was not recognized by anyone! People were running from her because she was frightening to them!

Clearwater Girl yelled out, "It is I, Clearwater Girl! Do not be afraid!"

With most of the juice washed from her hair, her beautiful blonde streak appeared again. She was so sad she had tried to change herself.

Her family was so happy she was not harmed. They had been worried when the storm had burst out of nowhere and they could not find her anywhere.

Clearwater Girl thought about all that had happened. She was just so happy to be herself again.

The sky cleared up, the sun came out, and the day was turning out to be a beautiful day after all. Her paint horse grazed in the sunlight.

Never had she been so happy to have that blonde streak and never again would she change it. She knew her family and friends loved her just the way she was!

From that day forward, she was very content to be who she was.

With the support of her family, Clearwater Girl accepted her differences, and would always be thankful for that beautiful blonde streak in her hair.

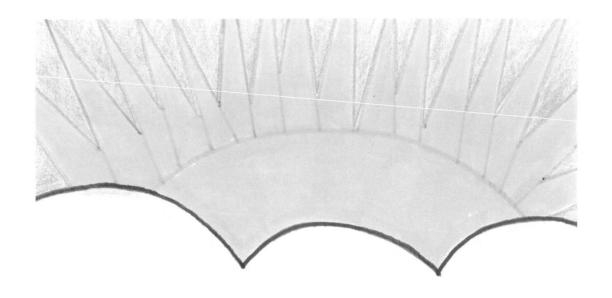

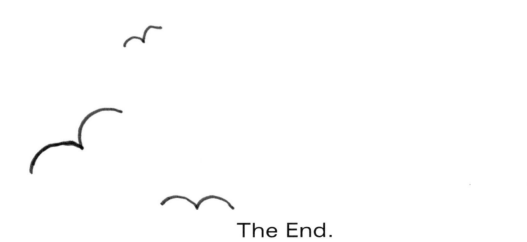

The End.

775709